Gabey the Bear

Baby Bear is So Special

By Elizabeth Hoover

Illustrated by Dakota Verrill

Published by Pen It! Publications, LLC in the U.S.A.

812-371-4128 www.penitpublications.com

ISBN: 978-1-954868-21-2

Illustrated by Dakota Verrill

Dedicated

To all those who have been part of our
Baby Bear's medical journey.

Our nurse, Cindy. Our Androscoggin Home
Health team: Kimlee, Carolyn, Marcie, Kim
and Dr. Sunday.

To all the staff, but especially our team at
Barbara Bush Children's Hospital.

Gabey Bear is so excited.
He is going to be a big brother!

Gabey Bear moves into his own room with his own really cool race car bed.

Momma and Daddy Bear get his old crib ready for Baby Bear.

Soon the day arrives.
Gabey Bear goes to Nana
and Papa Bear's house.

Momma and
Daddy Bear go
to the hospital
to bring home
Baby Bear.

When Gabey bear meets Baby Bear,
she is wearing a big pink bow. She is
so tiny! She is beautiful.
Baby Bear is special!

Momma Bear, Daddy Bear and Gabey Bear have a special treat: wild berries and honeycomb.

Baby Bear just has a bottle of milk. Baby Bear is special.

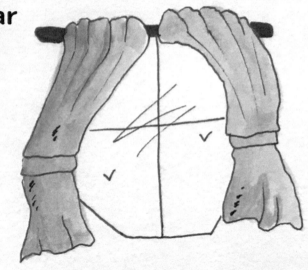

Early the next morning Momma Bear, Nana Bear,
Gabey Bear bring Baby Bear to the Big City.
Baby Bear has to see a doctor, called a Specialist,
because Baby Bear is special.

Gabey Bear likes to help feed Baby Bear her bottle.
But sometimes Baby Bear will cough and cough after she drinks. Momma Bear doesn't know why but says that Baby Bear is special.

One day, Momma and Daddy Bear have to go to the hospital in the Big City.

Gabey Bear can't go but they take Baby Bear, because Baby Bear is special.

When they come home from the hospital, Baby Bear doesn't drink from a bottle anymore. Baby Bear has a special tube that goes right to her stomach- because Baby Bear is special.

Gabey Bear learns new words like "Mickey Button", "g-tube", and "pumper".

He listens carefully so he can help because Baby Bear is special.

In the next few weeks many new bears start coming to their house. There is a Nurse Bear, Physical Therapy Bear, Occupational Therapy Bear, Speech Therapy Bear - Why? Because Baby Bear is special.

HOME · SWEET · HOME

As Baby Bear gets older, Physical Therapy Bear helps her to get special shoes and a walker just like Great Grampa Bear uses. So Baby Bear can learn how to walk because Baby Bear is special.

Shoes

"Thank You"

Baby Bear can't really talk so Momma Bear, Daddy Bear and Gabey Bear learn to sign.

"Love You"

"More"

They teach Sign Language to Baby Bear - because Baby Bear is special.

Gabey Bear has learned so much because of Baby Bear! He decides that some day he would like to be a doctor.

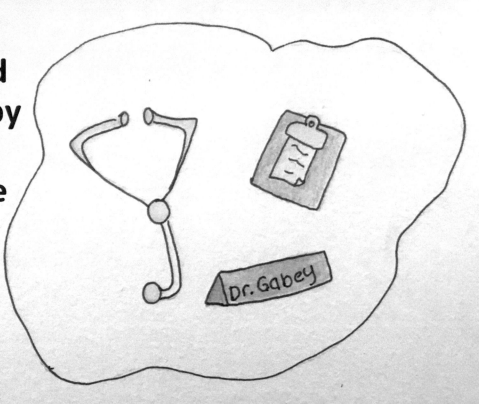

That way he could help all the baby Bears who are special.

 **Author Elizabeth (Beth) Hoover** is recently retired. She lives in an old Maine farmhouse with her husband, Steve. A dog, Molly and two bunnies, Olaf and Nala.

Daughter Marybeth and her husband TJ live nearby and "Nana Beth" delights in spending time with them and grand-children Gabe and Sammie.

Beth has a passion for teaching God's Word to children and has been involved has been doing this in some manner for over 40 years.

In her spare time Beth enjoys crafts, cooking and reading.

CPSIA information can be obtained
at www.ICGtesting.com
Printed in the USA
BVRC100859240621
610370BV00007B/339